W.H. Thomas

Some Current Folk-Songs of the Negro

Outlook

W.H. Thomas

Some Current Folk-Songs of the Negro

1. Auflage | ISBN: 978-3-73262-915-2

Erscheinungsort: Frankfurt am Main, Deutschland

Erscheinungsjahr: 2018

Outlook Verlag GmbH, Frankfurt.

SOME CURRENT FOLK-SONGS
OF THE NEGRO

BY
W. H. THOMAS, College Station, Texas

Read before the Folk-Lore Society of Texas, 1912

PUBLISHED BY THE FOLK-LORE SOCIETY OF TEXAS

WILL THOMAS AND THE TEXAS FOLK-LORE SOCIETY

Now that this brochure is being reprinted by the Texas Folk-Lore Society, I take the opportunity to say a word concerning its author and its history.

Although not a numbered publication, **Some Current Folk-Songs of the Negro** (1912) was the first item produced by the Texas Folk-Lore Society. At the time dues to the Society were two-bits a year—not enough to allow a very extensive publication. Number I (now reprinted under the title of **Round the Levee**) was not issued until 1916; then it was seven more years before another volume was issued, since which time, 1923, the Society has sent out a book annually to its members. The credit for initiating the Society's policy of recording the lore of Texas and the Southwest belongs to Will H. Thomas.

At the time his pamphlet was issued, he was president of the organization, to which office he was elected again in 1923. His idea was that people who work with folk-lore should not only collect it but interpret it and also enjoy it. This view is expressed in his delightful essay on "The Decline and Decadence of Folk Metaphor," in **Publications** Number II (**Coffee in the Gourd**) of the Society.

The view is thoroughly representative of the man, for Will Thomas was a vigorous, sane man with a vigorous, sane mind. He had a sense of humor and, therefore, a sense of the fitness of things. For nearly thirty years he taught English in the Agricultural and Mechanical College of Texas, and I have often wished that more professors of English in the colleges and universities over the country saw into the shams and futilities and sheer nonsense that passes for "scholarship" as thoroughly as he saw into them. Yet he was tolerant. He was a salt-of-the-earth kind of man.

He was born of the best of old-time Texas stock on a farm in Fayette County, January 11, 1880; he got his collegiate training at Austin College, Sherman, and the University of Texas and then took his Master's degree at Columbia University. He was co-editor, with Stewart Morgan, of two volumes of essays designed for collegians. He died March 1, 1935. Gates Thomas, Professor of English in Southwestern State Teachers College at San Marcos, who has done notable work in Negro folk songs and who is one of the nestors and pillars of the Texas Folk-Lore Society, is his brother.

J. FRANK DOBIE
Austin, Texas
April, 1936

SOME CURRENT FOLK-SONGS OF THE NEGRO AND THEIR ECONOMIC INTERPRETATION.

BY W. H. THOMAS, COLLEGE STATION, TEXAS.

Mr. President, Members of the Folk-Lore Society, Ladies and Gentlemen:

I should first like to say a word as to why I have been given the honor of addressing this meeting. Mr. Lomax is solely to blame for that. A short while after this society was organized, Mr. Lomax approached me one day while I was holding an examination and asked me to join the society and to make a study of the negro songs. He did so, no doubt, out of a knowledge of the fact that as I had lived all by life in a part of the State where the negroes are thick, and as I was then devoting my summers to active farming where negroes were employed, I would, therefore, have an excellent opportunity for studying the negro and his songs, as the geologist would say, *in situ*.

You will notice that I have taken as my title, "Some Current Folk-Songs of the Negro and Their Economic Interpretation." Now it is somewhat misleading at this day and time to speak of the negro as a "folk." That word seems to me to be applicable only to a people living in an industry in which economic function has not been specialized. So it would be more accurate to speak of "negro class lore." The class that I am treating of is the semi-rural proletariat. So far as my observation goes, the property-holding negro never sings. You see, property lends respectability, and respectability is too great a burden for any literature to bear, even our own. Although we generally think of beliefs, customs, and practices, when we hear the word "folk-lore" used, I believe all treatises on the subject recognize songs, sayings, ballads, and arts of all kinds as proper divisions of the subject. So a collection and study of the following songs is certainly not out of place on a program got up by this society.

Now just one word more under this head. I have found it very difficult to keep separate and distinct the study of folk-lore and the study of folk-psychology. The latter has always been extremely interesting to me; hence I can't refrain from sharing with you the two following instances: A negro girl was once attending a protracted meeting when she "got religion" and went off into a deep swoon, which lasted for two whole days, no food or drink being taken in the meantime. A negro explained to me as follows: "Now when that nigger comes to, if she's been possumin', she sho' will be hungry; but if she hasn't been possumin', it will be just the same as if she had been eatin' all the time." The other instance is that of an old negro who just before he died had been lucky enough to join a burial association which guaranteed to its members a relatively elaborate interment. So, when this old negro died, the undertaker dressed him out in a nice black suit, patent leather shoes, laundered shirt and collar, and all that. His daughter, in relating the incident after the funeral, said: "Bless your life, when they put Pappy in that coffin, he looked so fine that he just *had* to open his eyes and look at his self."

I imagine that folk-lore appeals differently to different individuals according to what intellectual or cultural interest predominates their beings. I suppose that the first interest in folk-lore was that of the antiquarian. Then came the interest of the linguist and the literateur. But it seems to me that if the pursuit of folk-lore is to be thoroughly worth while to-day the interest must above all be psychological and sociological. At least these are my interests in the subject. For instance, take that piece of well known folk-lore—the belief that by hanging a dead snake on a barbed wire fence—one can induce rain in a time of drought. I would give almost anything to know just how the two ideas "hanging a snake on a fence" and "raining" were ever associated. But I can perhaps still better illustrate my attitude by relating a piece of Herbert Spencerian lore. Herbert Spencer tells in his autobiography of this incident that he met with while on one of his annual trips to Scotland. The house at which he was a guest contained a room which bore the reputation of being haunted. It was in this room that Herbert Spencer was asked to sleep. So he did and lay awake most of the night, though not out of fear that the ghost would choose that particular night to pay a visit, but out of a philosophical curiosity to figure out the origin of such a "fool" belief.

In reference to these songs, when I say that I am interested in a study of origins, I do not mean the origin of any particular song, but the origin of the songs as a social phenomenon. Or to put it interrogatively, why do the members of this particular class sing, and why do their songs contain the thoughts that they do?

I believe it is pretty generally agreed today that any well-defined period of literature is merely the reflection of some great economic change. I notice that the critics have begun to speak of Victorian literature as merely the ornament of nineteenth century prosperity—the prosperity that was incident to the utilization of steam as motive power.

Now a great change has come into the negro's economic life within the past two decades. Its causes have been two. He has come into competition with the European immigrant, whose staying qualities are much greater than his; and agriculture has been changing from a feudalistic to a capitalistic basis, which requires a greater technical ability than the negro possesses. The result is that he is being steadily pushed into the less inviting and less secure occupations. To go into the intricacies of my thesis would be to abuse the privilege of the program; so I shall have to content myself with merely stating it. The negro, then, sings because he is losing his economic foothold. This economic insecurity has interfered most seriously with those two primal necessities— work and love—and you will notice that the thoughts in all these songs cluster around these two ideas.

So much for the interpretation; now for the appreciation. It has been my experience that where a knowledge of the negro's every day, or rather every-night, life is lacking, the appreciation of these songs is never very keen. Hence, in order to make it certain that you will appreciate these songs, I deem it necessary to try to acquaint you with the life of one of the "songsters." Otherwise I am afraid that too many of you will look upon these songs as absolutely puerile. Remember that a greater man than you or I once declared the ancient ballads to be without merit and also maintained that he could write, on the spur of the moment, a stanza that was just as good and that contained just as much meaning. Whereupon, being challenged he sat down and wrote:

"I put my hat upon my head and went into the Strand,
And there I met another man with his hat in his hand."

The colored semi-rural proletarian, then—how shall I describe him so that you may see him in your mind's eye, as I read these songs? I don't know how many of you are already acquainted with him, but, if any of you have ever tried to employ him profitably, I am sure you will never forget him. Perhaps I can picture him best by using the method of contrast. Let us follow one as he works with a white man, the latter, of course, being boss. We shall start with the morning.

The white man rises early and eats his breakfast. My proletarian doesn't rise at all for the chances are that he has never gone to bed. At noon they "knock off." While the white man is preparing to eat his lunch, the "nigger" has already done so and is up in the bed of a wagon or on a plank underneath a tree fast asleep, usually with his head in the sun. At nightfall, the white man eats supper and spends the evening reading or with his family. Not so my proletarian. He generally borrows thirty-five cents from the white man, steps out the back gate, gives a shrill whistle or two, and allows how he believes he'll "step off a piece to-night."

As I have not been on the farm much for the last two years. I have been unable to use the Boswellian method of recording these songs but have had to depend mostly on memory. The result is that some of them are not complete and some may not be textually correct. Of course the collection is not anything like an exhaustive one.

If you consider these songs as the negro's literature, you will notice some striking parallels between its history and that of English literature. As all of you know, English literature for several centuries was little more than paraphrases of various parts of the Bible. The first songs I shall read you are clearly not indigenous but are merely revamping the Biblical incidents and reflections of the sect disputes of the whites. The first song here presented is one that I heard twenty years ago as it was sung on the banks of a creek at a "big baptizing." It is entitled:

LL ALL THE MEMBERS I'M A NEW BORN.

I went to the valley on a cloudy day.
    O good Lord!
My soul got so happy that I couldn't get away.

        Chorus.

    Tell all the members I'm a new-born,
    I'm a new-born, I'm a new-born,
    O Lord!
    I'm a new-born baby, born in the manger,
    Tell all the members I'm a new-born.

Read the Scriptures, I am told,
Read about the garment Achan stole.

        Chorus.

Away over yonder in the harvest fields,
    O good Lord!
Angels working with the chariot wheels.

        Chorus.

Away over yonder, got nothing to do,
    O good Lord!
But to walk about Heaven and shout Halloo.

Chorus.

I'm so glad, I don't know what about,
   O good Lord!
Sprinkling and pourings done played out.

Chorus.

Here are two more of the same kind:

PREACHING IN THE WILDERNESS.

Daniel in that lion's den,
He called God A'mighty for to be his friend;
Read a little further, 'bout the latter clause:
The angel locked them lions' jaws.

Refrain.

   Oh, Daniel, hallelujah;
   Oh, Daniel, preaching in that wilderness.

Old man Adam, never been out;
Devil get in him, he'll jump up and shout;
He'll shout till he give a poor sister a blow,
Then he'll stop right still and he'll shout no more.

Refrain.

P's for peter; in his word
He tells us all not to judge;
Read a little further and you'll find it there,
I knows the tree by the fruit it bear.

Refrain.

VE ME FROM SINKING DOWN.

Seven stars in his right hand,
   Save me from sinking down.
All stars move at his command,
   Save me from sinking down.

Refrain.

, my Lord, save me from sinking down.

John was a Baptist, so am I,
   Save me from sinking down.
And he heard poor Israel's cry,
   Save us from sinking down.

The following is only a snatch, but it is enough to show that the economic factor was not yet predominant. In it we still see traces of the Bible's influence:

O Lord, sinner, you got to die,
   It may be to-day or to-morrow.
You can't tell the minute or the hour,
   But, sinner, you've got to die.

Refrain.

We now come to songs originated by the present generation of negroes. They all deal with work and love. The following might be entitled:

HE SONG OF THE FORTUNATE ONE.

The reason why I don't work so hard,
I got a gal in the white folks' yard;
And every night about half past eight,
I steps in through the white man's gate;
And she brings the butter, and the bread, and the lard;
That's the reason why I don't work so hard.

The next I have termed the "Skinner's Song." Skinner is the vernacular for teamster. The negro seldom carries a watch, but still uses the sun as a chronometer; a watch perhaps would be too suggestive of regularity. Picture to yourself several negroes working on a levee as teamsters. About five o'clock you would hear this:

I lookt at the sun and the sun lookt high;
I lookt at the Cap'n and he wunk his eye;
And he wunk his eye, and he wunk his eye,
I lookt at the Cap'n and he wunk his eye.

I lookt at the sun and the sun lookt red;
I lookt at the Cap'n and he turned his head;

And he turned his head, and he turned his head,
I lookt at the Cap'n and he turned his head.

The negro occasionally practices introspection. When he does, you are likely to hear something like this:

White folks are all time bragging,
   Lord, Lord, Lord,
'Bout a nigger ain't nothing but waggin,
   Lord, Lord, Lord.

Or,

White folks goes to college; niggers to the field;
White folks learn to read and write; niggers learn to steal.

Or,

Beauty's skin deep, but ugly's to the bone.
Beauty soon fades, but ugly holds its own.

The following is the only song in which I think I detect insincerity. Now the negro may have periods of despondency, but I have never been able to detect them.

THE RAILROAD BLUES.

I got the blues, but I haven't got the fare,
I got the blues, but I haven't got the fare,
  I got the blues, but I am too damn'd mean to cry.

Some folks say the rolling blues ain't bad;
Well, it must not 'a' been the blues my baby had.

Oh! where was you when the rolling mill burned down?
On the levee camp about fifteen miles from town

My mother's dead, my sister's gone astray,
And that is why this poor boy is here to-day.

If any of you have high ideas about the universal sacredness of domestic ties, prepare to shed them now. It has often been said that the negro is a backward race. But this is not true. In fact, he is very forward. He had invented trial marriage before sociology was a science.

The following songs are only too realistic:

FIRST.

I dreamt last night I was walking around,
I met that nigger and I knocked her down;
I knocked her down and I started to run,
Till the sheriff done stopped me with his Gatling gun.

I made a good run, but I run too slow,
He landed me over in the Jericho;
I started to run off down the track,
But they put me on the train and brought me back.

SECOND.

Says, when I die,
   Bury me in black,
For if you love that of woman of mine,
   I'll come a sneakin' back;
For if you love that woman of mine,
   I'll come a sneakin' back.

THIRD.

If you don't quit monkeying with my Lulu,
   I'll tell you what I'll do;
I'll fling around your heart with my razor;
   I'll shoot you through and through.

That the negro's esthetic nature may be improving is indicated by the following song. For tremendousness of comparison, I know nothing to equal it. It is entitled:

THE BROWN-SKINNED WOMAN.

A brown-skinned woman and she's chocolate to the bone.
A brown-skinned woman and she smells like toilet soap.
A black-skinned woman and she smells like a billy goat.
A brown-skinned woman makes a freight train slip and slide.
A brown-skinned woman makes an engine stop and blow.
A brown-skinned woman makes a bulldog break his chain.
A brown-skinned woman makes a preacher lay his Bible down.
I married a woman; she was even tailor made.

You will find plenty of economics in the following song. The present-day negro early made that most fatal of all discoveries: namely, that a man can really live in this world without working. Hence his *beau ideal* is the gambler, and his *bête noir* is the county jail or the penitentiary.

THE GAMBLER'S PANTS.

What kind of pants does a gambler wear?
Great big stripes, cost nine a pair.

JACK O' DIAMONDS.

Jack o' Diamonds, Jack o' Diamonds,
Jack o' Diamonds is a hard card to roll.

Says, whenever I gets in jail,
Jack o' Diamonds goes my bail;
And I never, Lord, I never,
Lord, I never was so hard up before.

You may work me in the winter,
You may work me in the fall;
I'll get e-ven, I'll get e-ven,
I'll get even through that long summer's day.

Jack o' Diamonds took my money,
And the piker got my clothes;
And I ne-e-ver, and I ne-e-ver,
Lord, I never was so hard run before.

Says, whenever I gets in jail,
I'se got a Cap'n goes my bail;
And a Lu-u-la, and a Lu-u-la,
And a Lulu that's a hard-working chile.

TO HUNTSVILLE.

The jurymen found me guilty, the judge he did say:
    "This man's convicted to Huntsville, poor boy,
For ten long years to stay."

My mammy said, "It's a pity." My woman she did say:
    "They're taking my man to Huntsville, poor boy,
For ten long years to stay."

Upon that station platform we all stood waiting that day,
    Awaiting that train for Huntsville, poor boy,
For ten long years to stay.

The train ran into the station, the sheriff he did say:
    "Get on this train for Huntsville, poor boy,
For ten long years to stay."

Now, if you see my Lula, please tell her for me,
    I've done quit drinking and gambling, poorboy,
And getting on my sprees.

DON'T LET YOUR WATCH RUN DOWN, CAP'N.

Working on the section, dollar and a half a day,
    Working for my Lula; getting more thanpay, Cap'n,
Getting more than pay.

Working on the railroad, mud up to my knees,
    Working for my Lula; she's a hard old girl to please, Cap'n,
She's a hard girl to please.
    So don't let your watch run down, Cap'n,
    Don't let your watch run down.

BABY, TAKE A LOOK AT ME.

I went to the jail house and fell on my knees,
The first thing I noticed was a big pan of peas.
The peas was hard and the bacon was fat;
Says, your oughter seen the niggers that was grabbin' at that.

Refrain.

Oh, Lord, Baby, take a look at me!

Brandy, whisky, Devil's Island gin,
Doctor said it would kill him, but he didn't tell him when.

Refrain.

Oh, Lord, Baby, take a look at me!

DON'T YOU LEAVE ME HERE.

Don't you leave me here, don't you leave me here,
For if you leave me here, babe, they'll arrest me sure.

They'll arrest me sure.
For if you leave me here, babe, they'll arrest me sure.

Don't leave me here, don't leave me here,
For if you leave me here, you'll leave a dime for beer.

Why don't you be like me, why don't you be like me?
Quit drinking whisky, babe, let the cocaine be.

It's a mean man that won't treat his woman right.

The following is a tragedy in nine acts:

FRANKIE.

Frankie was a good girl, as everybody knows,
She paid a hundred dollars for Albert a suit of clothes;
He was her man, babe, but she shot him down.

Frankie went to the bar-keeper's to get a bottle of beer;
She says to the bar-keeper: "Has my living babe been here?"
He was her man, babe, but he done her wrong.

The bar-keeper says to Frankie: "I ain't going to tell you no lie,
Albert passed 'long here walking about an hour ago with a nigger named Alkali."
He was her man, babe, but he done her wrong.

Frankie went to Albert's house; she didn't go for fun;
For, underneath her apron was a blue-barrel 41.
He was her man, babe, but he done her wrong.

When Frankie got to Albert's house, she didn't say a word,
But she cut down upon poor Albert just like he was a bird.
He was her man, babe, but she shot him down.

When Frankie left Albert's house, she lit out in a run,
For, underneath her apron was a smoking 41.
He was her man, babe, but he done her wrong.

"Roll me over, doctor, roll me over slow,
Cause, when you rolls me over, them bullets hurt me so;
I was her man, babe, but she shot me down."

Frankie went to the church house and fell upon her knees,
Crying "Lord 'a' mercy, won't you give my heart some ease?
He was my man, babe, but I shot him down."

Rubber-tired buggy, decorated hack,
They took him to the graveyard, but they couldn't bring him back.
He was her man, babe, but he done her wrong.

And, once more, the female of the species was more deadly than the male.

www.ingramcontent.com/pod-product-compliance
Lightning Source LLC
Chambersburg PA
CBHW080731250626
47170CB00011B/2901